YALNIZ BALİNA

Benji Davies

Çeviren: Oğuzhan Aydın

REDHOUSE
kidz

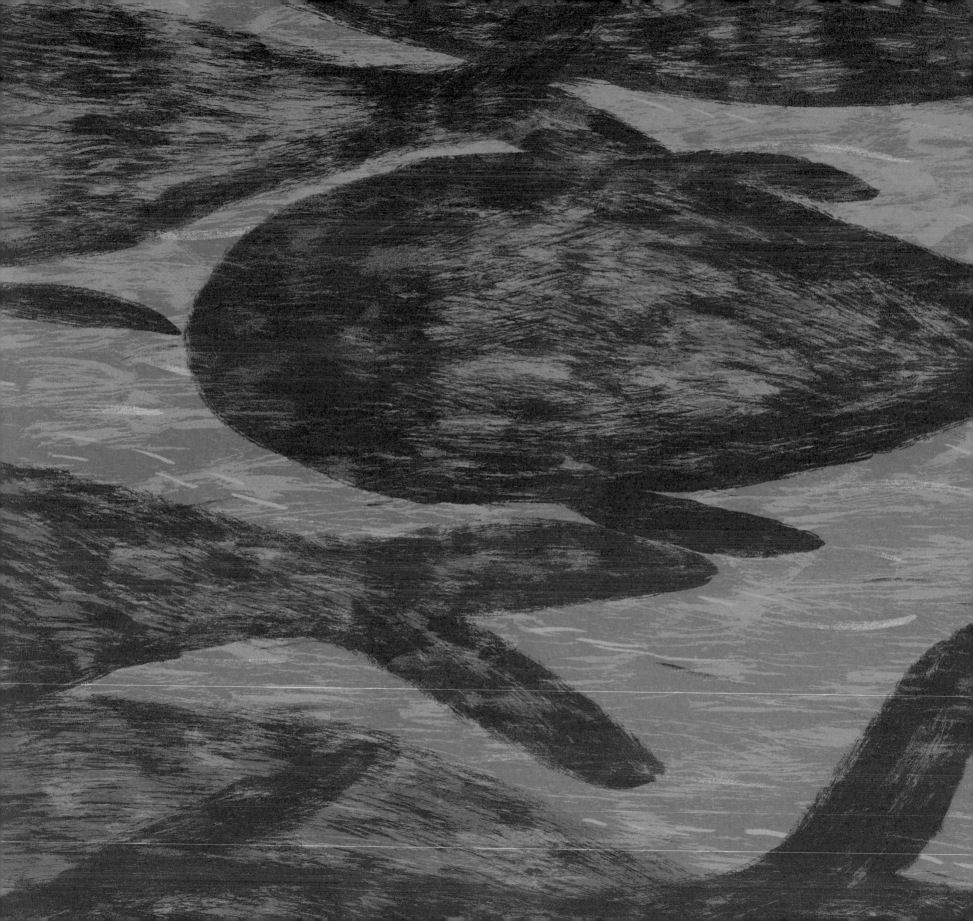

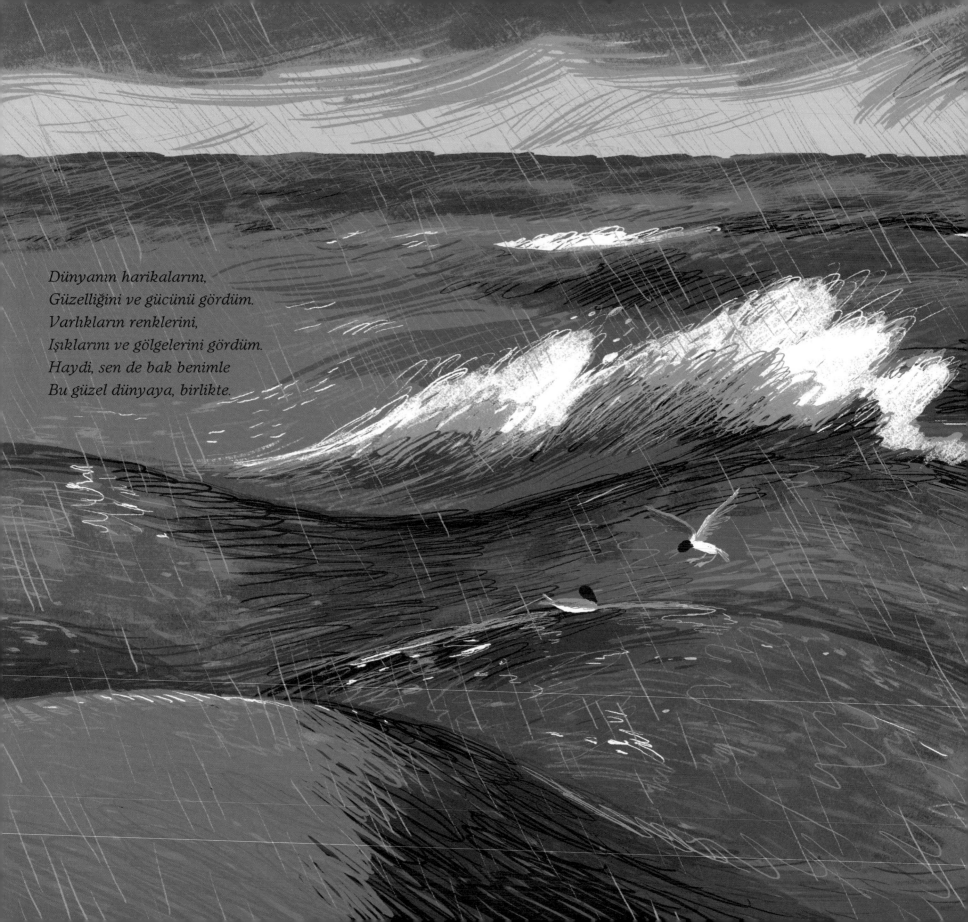

Dünyanın harikalarını,
Güzelliğini ve gücünü gördüm.
Varlıkların renklerini,
Işıklarını ve gölgelerini gördüm.
Haydi, sen de bak benimle
Bu güzel dünyaya, birlikte.

YALNIZ BALINA

Benji Davies

REDHOUSE
kidz

Noi, babası ve altı kedisiyle birlikte deniz kenarında yaşıyordu.

Babası her gün sabah erkenden kalkar,
kayığına binip bütün gün balık tutardı.

Hava kararana kadar eve dönmezdi.

Bir gece, evlerinin yakınlarında büyük bir fırtına koptu.

Sabah olunca Noi, fırtınanın geride neler bıraktığını görmek için kumsala indi.

Deniz kenarında yürürken
uzakta bir şey gördü.

Gördüğü şeye yaklaştıkça gözlerine inanamadı.

Bu, kıyıya vurmuş küçük bir balinaydı.

Noi ne yapması gerektiğini düşündü.

Balinaların karada yaşayamayacağını
biliyordu.

"Acele etmeliyim!" diye düşündü.

Noi, balinanın yabancılık çekmemesi için
elinden gelen her şeyi yaptı.

Ona ada hayatıyla ilgili hikâyeler anlattı.
Balina çok iyi bir dinleyiciydi.

Akşam olmak üzereydi,
hava kararmaya başlamıştı.

Babası küvetteki balinayı görünce
kızacak diye endişeleniyordu Noi.

Her nasılsa Noi sırrını
bütün gece sakladı.

Hatta bir ara balinasına gizlice
yemek bile götürdü.

Ama bunun sonsuza kadar
süremeyeceğini biliyordu.

Noi'nin babası kızmamıştı.
İşiyle her zaman o kadar meşguldü ki
Noi'nin yalnız olduğunu fark etmemişti.

Ancak balinayı ait olduğu yere, denize
geri götürmeleri gerektiğini söyledi.

Noi yapmaları gerekenin bu olduğunu
biliyordu, yine de veda etmek zordu.

İyi ki babası yanındaydı.

Noi'nin aklına sık sık yalnız balina geliyordu.

Belki bir gün…

...arkadaşını yine görürdü.

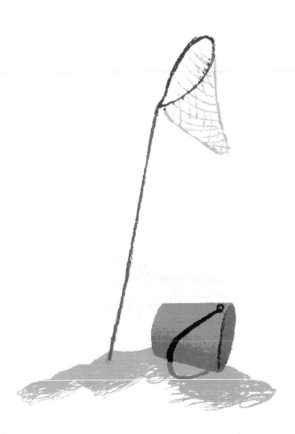

SEV Yayıncılık Eğitim ve Ticaret A.Ş.
bir Sağlık ve Eğitim Vakfı kuruluşudur.
Nuhkuyusu Cad., No. 197 Üsküdar İş Merkezi, Kat 3, 34664
Bağlarbaşı, Üsküdar, İstanbul
Tel.: (0216) 474 23 43 • Sertifika No. 45278

Yalnız Balina

Metin ve Resimler: © 2013 Benji Davies
Orijinal Eser: © 2013 Simon & Schuster UK Ltd
1st Floor, 222 Gray's Inn Road, London, WC1X 8HB
A CBS Company
Türkçe Çeviri: © 2017 SEV Yayıncılık Eğitim ve Ticaret A.Ş.
Türkçe baskısı Simon & Schuster'in izni ile yayımlanmıştır.

Yazan ve Resimleyen: Benji Davies
Özgün Adı: The Storm Whale
Çeviren: Oğuzhan Aydın
Yayın Yönetmeni: S. Baha Sönmez
Editör: Burcu Ünsal Çeküç
Son Okuma: Gökçe Ateş Aytuğ
Baskıya Hazırlayan: Hüseyin Vatan

Birinci Baskı: Haziran 2017
Yedinci Baskı: Aralık 2022
ISBN: 978-605-9781-57-2

For Karen, who chose Lupin from
The Wainwright Shelter, Animal Rescue Cumbria, 1990
~

J.L.

First published in Great Britain in 2000 by
Frances Lincoln Limited, 4 Torriano Mews,
Torriano Avenue, London NW5 2RZ

British Library Cataloguing in Publication Data available on request

ISBN 0-7112-1542-1 hardback
ISBN 0-7112-1543-X paperback

Printed in Hong Kong

1 3 5 7 9 8 6 4 2

MISSING!

Jonathan Langley

FRANCES LINCOLN

When Daisy went to nursery ...

... Lupin stayed at home.

JONATHAN LANGLEY studied at the Liverpool College of Art
and the Central School of Art and Design.
A hugely successful author/illustrator of children's books,
his titles have sold over a million copies throughout the world.
They include the *Collins Book of Nursery Rhymes*,
The Bedtime Treasury and *Nursery Tales* books (HarperCollins).
Jonathan lives in the Lake District with his wife,
two children and Lupin the cat.

After nursery Lupin would meet Daisy on the corner
at the end of their road.

When the holidays started, Daisy didn't go to nursery ...

... but Lupin didn't know.

Daisy was busy all morning ...

... and so was Lupin.

Lupin went for his morning stroll

and arrived at the corner at the usual time.

Daisy hung up her painting, then looked for Lupin.
"Time for your fishy biscuits, Lupin!" she called.

Lupin waited at the corner.

'Where is Daisy?' he wondered. 'Has she gone on a school trip?
Or to a birthday party? When is she coming back?'

Daisy looked in Lupin's favourite places,
but she couldn't find him anywhere.
"Where are you, Lupin?" Daisy called.

Lupin wandered along the road towards Nursery. Sudde
Lupin raced back to the corner. 'Perhaps a

Daisy looked everywhere. "What if a lion

og leapt out of a gateway and barked at him.

g has chased Daisy away!' he thought.

ased Lupin away! Or a shark! Oh no!" she cried.

Lupin ran to the top of the tree. He looked ou

'What if a big bird has carried Da

Daisy hunted for lions and sharks, but there were none to

'Has he been turned into a frog

as he could see, but there was no sign of Daisy.
' he thought. 'I must rescue her!'

ı. 'Has Lupin been stolen by a wicked witch?' she thought.
ced up in a tower? I must rescue him!'

'What has happened to Daisy?' Lupin thought.
'Is she lost? Is she all alone and can't find her way home?'

Daisy looked out of her window across the town.
   'Is Lupin lost?' she wondered. 'Is he all alone
and can't find his way home?'

'Daisy has gone away,' thought Lupin. 'Perhaps sh

"Lupin has gone away," said Daisy. "Perhaps I did

ne to live somewhere else. Perhaps she's got a new cat.'

d him enough. Perhaps he's found a new home."

'Lupin doesn't love me any mo

...but I must do something spec

ught Daisy. 'He's never coming back ...

t in case he does come back.'

Lupin went round to the back of the house. It was v

'... but perhaps she's left me a little

et. 'Daisy doesn't love me any more,' he thought ...

food. What's that in my basket?'

"Lupin!"

"WHERE HAVE YOU BEEN?!"

MORE PICTURE BOOKS AVAILABLE IN PAPERBACK FROM FRANCES LINCOLN

Ellie's Growl

Karen Popham

Ellie likes it when her big brother William reads her stories about animals, because he makes wonderful animal noises... An exuberant read-aloud picture book for young children, with enchanting illustrations.

Suitable for Nursery Education and for National Curriculum English – Reading, Key Stage 1
Scottish Guidelines English Language – Reading, Level A

ISBN 0-7112-1505-7 £4.99

Simon Says!

Shen Roddie

Illustrated by Sally Anne Lambert

Simon Pig has the perfect plan to make Sally Goose do all his work. "Let's play Simon Says!" he says to her. "You do whatever Simon Says..."

Suitable for National Curriculum English – Reading, Key Stage 1
Scottish Guidelines English Language – Reading, Level A

ISBN 0-7112-1532-4 £5.99

The Egg

Mark Robertson

When George discovers a rather large egg under his mother's favourite chicken, he soon finds himself looking after a baby dragon. But the dragon begins pining for his own kind, and one day he disappears.

Suitable for National Curriculum English – Reading, Key Stages 1 and 2
Scottish Guidelines English Language – Reading, Levels A and B

ISBN 0-7112-1671-1 £5.99

Frances Lincoln titles are available from all good bookshops.
Prices are correct at time of publication, but may be subject to change.